Hi I'm Feely and this is my diary.

There are six Feely books so far. It's best to

read them in this order:

1   Feely's Magic Diary

2   Feely for Prime Minister

3   Feely and Her Well-Mad Parents

4   Feely Goes to Work

5   Feely and Henry VIII

6   Feely and Someone Else's Granny

Feely for Prime Minister
by Barbara Catchpole
Illustrated by Jan Dolby

Published by Ransom Publishing Ltd.
Unit 7, Brocklands Farm, West Meon, Hampshire GU32 IJN, UK
www.ransom.co.uk

ISBN   978 1785911 122 4
First published in 2016

Feely
for
Prime
Minister

Barbara Catchpole

Illustrated by Jan Dolby

Ransom

Monday

Dear Diary

I have some news! We are going to have a class Prime Minister!

My teacher, Miss Rosy, (smiles a lot, I mean a *lot*, quite nice, bit useless) says that in America they have class presidents.

So we are going to have a class Prime Minister. I expect it's just a Super Class Monitor really. (That would be a really rubbish superhero! 'Is it a bird? Is it a plane?

No, it's Super Class Monitor, saving the

world by giving out the pencils!')

I go to a huge school now. Mostly it's

made of glass. In winter it's freezing. In

summer they say it's boiling and everyone

goes red like tomatoes in a greenhouse.

The windows don't open. It's to stop us

jumping out or pushing each other out,

I suppose. But you *can* get them open a

little bit and chuck stuff out through the slit.

Saffron threw all Maria's books out last week, one at a time, because Maria 'looked at her'. Saffron is poison!

Anyway, that's just one thing that's wrong with my school. Don't get me started on the rest! You'd think grown-ups would do a better job!

My class is 7RP. The RP stands for Rosa

Parks. I am glad our class is named after her because:

a.   she was a woman (duh!) and

b.   she was quite stroppy.

Anyway Miss Rosy, our teacher (I'm sure she's my teacher, but she doesn't seem sure I'm in her class) stood up and clapped her hands three times.

We're all supposed to be silent then, but usually we can't hear her clapping because we're making too much noise.

She said:

'OK, listen up! No, quiet please! It's your own time you're wasting! Kylie, put your brush away! Is that a mobile? I want silence right away!'

Anyway, I'll cut out the first five minutes of her saying stuff because she didn't say anything (you know what I mean). → horrible

Here's the important bit:

'WILL YOU BE QUIET? Thank you!

Mrs Harding has this brilliant project. We do it every year. It's just genius! So much fun and so much to learn! I am mega-excited!

'We are going to have a – wait for it – a student leader for our class – a sort of Prime Minister.

'Saffron – put your hand down, honey. We are going to vote for whoever we think will do it best. So exciting! Everyone will vote.   VOTE

'Yes, Shane you *have* to do it. Because

Mrs Harding said so. If you can't be polite, go and stand outside the door! If you want to 'stand' and be a 'candidate' (she did that daft wiggly thing with her fingers) come and see me tomorrow and 'register' (more wiggling). It will be amaze-balls!'

Honestly, she thinks she's about twelve! She gave us a big smile, showing her huge teeth. They are really big – I'm not being

mean but they are huge.
Perhaps she can't even
close her mouth properly.
If they were mine, I'd get
them fixed.

Nope, I thought.

Not doing that. No

way!

Miss Rosy

thought playing a

musical instrument would be 'totally

awesome' (wiggly fingers) and look how *that*

turned out.

My cello is blooming impossible to play

and it takes a fork-lift to move it. One day

it'll fall on me and I won't be able to get up.

I'll probably starve to death — the first

person to be killed in a cello avalanche.

I have cello lessons each Friday and on

those days Mum has to drive me to school.

She moans all the way because she'll be

late for work ('Why couldn't you play the

harmonica?') and all the sad people will get

sadder.

Mum is a counsellor for sad and angry people. I expect the angry people get angrier too. I know I would. I hate having to wait for stuff.

Anyway, what was I saying? I know — I didn't want to be RPPM (Rosa Parks Prime Minister). I *knew* it was a trap.

HORRIBLE

At dinner (Mum makes us have dinner together once a week so we can 'touch

base', whatever that is) we had mac and

cheese. Mum cooked it.

Mine was like a house brick. I got really

tired trying to hack a bit off. Seriously, my

wrist started to hurt. Mac and cheese is

not supposed to be crunchy, right?

So I had a bit of a rest to get the

strength back in my arm, and told my

family about the voting thing. VOTE

This is what they said:

Mum:

'Oh, Feely, darling –
I think you should do it.
It would be such a positive thing. You *are* a
teensy bit negative, sweetie.'

Mum is quite hard to understand, so I'll
put it into English for you:

'Do it! It will stop you whinging!'

Dad said:

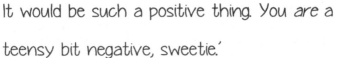

'You *would* learn a lot, Feely.'

He's a teacher and
'learning a lot' is important
to him.

I'm eleven and learn stuff all day. I try not to, but the grown-ups just ram it all into my head.

We even sing Maths rhymes in the dinner queue. Sometimes I just think my head will explode. Boom! Brains everywhere!

Or maybe, as they put new stuff in, old stuff falls out. One day I'll wake up knowing how to speak Spanish, but I won't remember any English. Or who my family are.

I'll have to go and live with a Spanish family (I won't know who they are, either!). At least the food will be better.

Anyway, Dad didn't say much because he had got a bit of mac and cheese in his mouth and was trying to get it soft enough to get rid of it.

I was just sucking mine – I didn't want to lose a tooth.

Ollie, my big brother, was trying to break his up by jabbing his fork up and down into it. Bits kept flying across the table.

Ollie said:

'Do it, Feely! Kevin Foss did it last year and he got to stay in when it rained at break.'

That made me think. Our teachers don't let us stay in for wet break unless we have a monsoon (loads of rain all at once) AND a tsunami (giant wave) AND frogs fall from the sky. All at the same time.

Perhaps it was worth being PM to stay in at break.

Tuesday

Yes! Yes! I would do it! I went to see Miss

Rosy in her little glass tank.

'Oh, Sally,'

she said.

'Phoebe.'

'I'm so glad!

It will be

brilliant!'

Turns out nobody else wanted to do it

and Miss thought she would have to tell

Mrs Harding. She said Class 7 Sherpa

Tenzing already had ten candidates.

'Thank you so much, er ... '

'Phoebe.'

I had to think of five things I would change about the school (no problem, there were zillions).

I had to make some posters, talk to people and make a speech. Then, because I was the only person anyway, I would be Prime Minister. Piece of cake!

Except ... Diary, this really, really, really sucks ... Saffron saw me leaving Miss Rosy in the Glass Box.

I heard her

talking later in her loud and squeaky voice.

We were in the dinner queue and I am sure

she wanted me to hear:

'I wasn't going to do it because

I thought, like, it was like, totally lame! But

then I heard that Feely Tonks – the

geekette with the glasses – the chubster

with the cello – well she was going to do it

and I thought, well, you know, like it was my

duty to win it.

'Because we don't want *her*, do we girls?'

I tried to look as if I didn't hear it but, honestly, you could hear them for miles.

She and her friends are called the Pink Click – they are a little gang.

They all laughed silly laughs and turned round to look at me. I went red and I could feel I wanted to cry, but it was weird because, at the same time, I was angry.

I was going to beat her. I was going to do it!

Wednesday

Today we 'campaigned' (wiggly fingers). That means we had to get people to vote for us. That is not as easy as you'd think, let me tell you! People are weird.

We had to promise to do things for the class. Linda Tatlow asked if she could have a pony. As if I were Santa!

Harry asked if he could meet Dannii Minogue.

No! I am not Father Christmas or some sort of giant blue genie! Anyway ...

Posters

Me:

Drama Club made me loads of posters.
They moaned a bit (this is not what Drama
Club is for) but I think they enjoyed the
colouring in.

They drew a nice picture of me. I took
my glasses off for it.

Saffron:

Took a selfie with the slogan: 'Vote for me! I'm awesome!'

Her mother printed hundreds of the things on Tuesday night at Staples.

There are still loads of them blowing around the playground.

Someone drew moustaches on all my lovely posters. I'm not saying it was the Pink Click, but all the moustaches were pink.

— HORRIBLE —

Talking to people

Me:

When I talked to people I noticed their eyes sort of went funny and they tried to edge away from me. They looked like crabs

who knew they had done something very wrong.

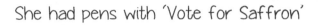

Saffron:

She had pens with 'Vote for Saffron'

on them. Posters *and* pens! How did she do that? Her mum is awesome.

And she put her 'Things to change' up on Facebook. Everybody saw it because I am, like, the only kid in the whole school not allowed on Facebook.

I asked Dad if I could do it this one time and he said, 'Not on your life, young lady' and went on marking.

I asked Mum and she said, 'You don't need social media to validate yourself, Feely.'

That meant 'No'.

Saffron's mum even tweeted! She used #Saffrules!

Other Stuff

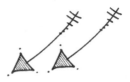

Saffron brought sweets in for everyone.
She said it was her birthday, but it wasn't.
She doesn't have a birthday – she was
made in a lab!

Now I have
the evening to
think of things
that I would
change at school
and to write my
speech.

I can still get this back – can't I?

I couldn't bear it if Saffron won. It would be just horrible.

 # Thursday

'When I win this thing, you are going to have to sharpen the pencils forever!'

Saffron sort of hissed at me and gave me a little pinch. It was just a tiny pinch but it left a mark.

(To be fair I enjoy sharpening pencils. You get to use the machine thing on Miss Rosy's desk.

Sometimes Shane feeds whole pencils into that thing!)

Still, I think Saffron is nuts!

We were in the corridor together before giving our speeches to the class.

I had worked hard on mine during the adverts last night. I went in first.

Here's my speech – I've copied it out for you.

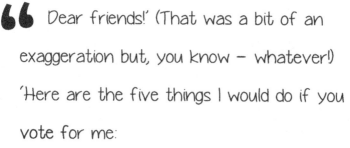 Dear friends!' (That was a bit of an exaggeration but, you know – whatever!) 'Here are the five things I would do if you vote for me:

 1. New stuff for the Drama Club (I had to promise them that to get them to do the posters for me.)

2. More Harry Potter books for the library.

 3. No homework to be handed in on Mondays. I say: give us the weekends off, like everyone else!

 4. An electric fan for our classroom in summer!

 5. More chips more often.

A vote for Feely is a good way to feel good. 🎙

VOTE VOTE

Daffy and Stacey – Saffron's gang – did the loud yawning thing all the way through my speech and fanned their hands in front of their mouths.

When I finished there was dead quiet. Then the Drama Club clapped a bit, and Shane said, 'Yeah! More chips! More chips!'

Saffron came in to give her speech. She

stood up on a chair (wish I'd thought to do

that).

Vote for your
PRIME
MINISTER!

She did her stupid giggle a couple of

times and said:

'Hi guys! Well you know I just love you

all and I'll give you everything you want.

Here are my five things:

1   A chocolate fountain in the

playground. If I invited you to my party, you'll know chocolate fountains rock! If I didn't invite you — I will do next

time — except you, Feely, of course.

2. Ice cream sundaes in the canteen every day and none of that chocolate pudding that just tastes brown that Mrs Roberts always does. Chips every single day!'

(That's three things!)

3. 'No homework at all — ever!

I know that won't make any
difference to some of you – ha! ha!'
(I just hate her silly giggle!)

4.   No more cross-country runs.
And mobile phones
allowed in class!'
(Two things! I put
my hand up, but
Miss Rosy ignored
me.)

5.   Longer summer holidays, so
I can go skiing as well as going to
our house in France.

Remember! A vote for Saffy is a vote
for fun!'   VOTE VOTE

She is never, NEVER called 'Saffy'! Also I was a bit annoyed that we went to Butlins at Skegness last year for a week, not skiing with royal people.

I had a great time though, apart from the day the sun came out and surprised us and I got burned.

Where was I? Oh yes — Daffy and

Stacy yelled 'Go Saffron!' (not 'Saffy' you notice) and 'Dead right' all the way through and everyone clapped like mad.

Shane was very worked up and thumped his desk, shouting, 'Chips! Chips! Chips!'

chips

chips

The Voting

VOTE

We all had bits of paper to mark our votes on. We had to put them in a big box with a slot in it on Miss Rosy's desk.

I carefully put a big cross next to Saffron because I didn't want her!

I VOTE FOR
☐ Phoebe
☒ Saffron
for Prime Minister

Then Miss Rosy started to count the votes and it was silent in the classroom. Even Shane was quietly writing something on his desk (or carving really — with a compass).

Miss Rosy carefully made a pile of votes and then Saffron and I had to go and stand at the front.

Still quiet. Very, very, quiet.

'I declare Saffron West to be our Prime

Minister!' Miss Rosy said. There was loads of

cheering and shouting.

I felt awful — like I would rather be

anywhere else.

Then it got worse ...

'How may votes did I get?' Saffron

asked. 'How many votes did Feely get?'

'It doesn't really matter,' said Miss Rosy.

'No,' Saffron said very, very loudly. 'You've got to say — they always say.'

'Well,' said Miss Rosy (she had gone a bit red), 'you got all the votes but one.'

So the Drama Club didn't even vote for me? Or Kaili who likes Harry Potter? I was so embarrassed!

'So,' said Saffron, really clearly, 'Feely got just one vote?'

'No,' Miss Rosy mumbled. 'One vote had a picture of Bart Simpson on it, so that didn't count.'

'Ha! Ha!' said Shane.

I just wanted to run away and never
ever come back to school.

 Friday

Today at lunchtime Saffron had a whole
bowl of yoghurt emptied on her head.

Dear Diary, let me tell you what
happened. It was totally hilarious.

First of all she comes in like Queen
Saffron the First with a big pink sparkly
badge which says: Official Prime Minister.

Then she orders me to sharpen the pencils.

All morning people want to know when the chocolate fountain is coming.

Now at lunchtime Saffron is eating and Shane comes up to her with his bowl full of strawberry yoghurt.

'Eh, Saffron,' he says. 'Can I talk to
you?'

I like Shane. He's not the brightest light
on the Christmas tree but he's nice.
Saffron looked at him as if he was muck
on her shoe.

'I'm eating now!' she said. 'Laters!'

'Thing is, Saffron. You promised me stuff. You said I could have an Arsenal shirt. And there would be a chocolate fountain.

'We didn't even have chips today and it's Friday. We always have chips on a Friday, but Mrs Roberts says we're not going to have chips because she's so upset someone insulted her chocolate pudding.

'And Linda hasn't got her pony. And this ... this ... '

I had never heard Shane talk so much. He was getting well stressed.

'This is not ice cream. This stuff is not ice cream. We got no ice cream!'

He was almost shouting by now and the canteen went quiet.

'Go away, Shane!' Saffron said, still shovelling food into her mouth.

'All that stuff isn't

going to happen! It was just pretend to get you to vote for me. I knew the teachers wouldn't do all that stuff. Are you stupid? Just bog off!'

Everybody gasped – no chocolate fountain!

Shane went red and looked at the bowl of goo in his hand and looked at Saffron and looked at the bowl again and looked at Saffron again.

It seemed like slow motion. Then he just turned the bowl upside down on her head.

'Pretend! Pretend! That's lying! Well, pretend that's shampoo!' he yelled and ran off (they caught him behind the bike shed).

Saffron just sat there with yoghurt dripping down her face and a strawberry on her nose!

I nearly wet myself trying not to laugh,

but then I saw everyone else was laughing and clapping.

Saffron burst into tears.

'Miss Rosy, Miss Rosy,' she sobbed, 'I don't want to be Prime Minister any more!'

I told Dad and he said, 'A week is a long time in politics, honey.'

I don't know what that means. My parents aren't very clear sometimes.

But I do know one thing: I'm not doing it! It's a rubbish job!

About the author

Barbara Catchpole was a teacher for thirty years and enjoyed every minute. She has three sons of her own who were always perfectly behaved and never gave her a second of worry.

Barbara also tells lies.

How many have you read?

Feely's Magic Diary
Barbara Catchpole

Feely for Prime Minister
Barbara Catchpole

Feely and her Well-Mad Parents
Barbara Catchpole

How many have you read?

Goes to Work

and Henry VIII
Barbara Catchpole

and Someone Else's Granny
Barbara Catchpole

Have you met  **PIG**?

Meet P.I.G – Peter Ian Green, although everybody calls him PIG for short. PIG lives with his mum.

He is small for his age, but says his mum is huge for hers. She is a single mum, but PIG says she looks more like a double mum or even a treble mum.

PIG and the Ice-cream Cake
Barbara Catchpole

PIG Skives off School
Barbara Catchpole

PIG is a Blue Baboon's Bottom
Barbara Catchpole

PIG SuperPig!
Barbara Catchpole

PIG and the Baldy Cat
Barbara Catchpole

PIG Leaves Home (for a bit)
Barbara Catchpole

PIG Whopping Great Fib
Barbara Catchpole

PIG is Harry Snotter
Barbara Catchpole

PIG and the Rainbow Hair
Barbara Catchpole

PIG and the Big Quiz
Barbara Catchpole

PIG Gets Angry
Barbara Catchpole

PIG's Season's Finale
Barbara Catchpole